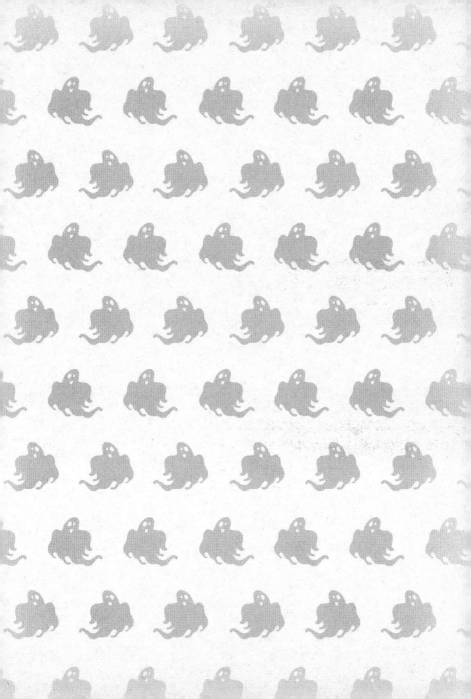

DESMOND COLE
GHOST PATROL

MAJOR MONSTER MESS

by **Andres Miedoso**
illustrated by **Victor Rivas**

LITTLE SIMON
New York   London   Toronto   Sydney   New Delhi

LITTLE SIMON
An imprint of
Simon & Schuster Children's Publishing Division
1230 Avenue of the Americas, New York, New York 10020
First Little Simon hardcover edition November 2018
Copyright © 2018 by Simon & Schuster, Inc.
Also available in a Little Simon paperback edition.
All rights reserved, including the right of reproduction
in whole or in part in any form.
LITTLE SIMON is a registered trademark of Simon & Schuster, Inc.,
and associated colophon is a trademark of Simon & Schuster, Inc.
For information about special discounts for bulk purchases, please contact
Simon & Schuster Special Sales at 1-866-506-1949 or
business@simonandschuster.com.
The Simon & Schuster Speakers Bureau can bring authors to your
live event. For more information or to book an event contact the
Simon & Schuster Speakers Bureau at 1-866-248-3049
or visit our website at www.simonspeakers.com.
Designed by Steve Scott
Manufactured in the United States of America 1018 FFG
2 4 6 8 10 9 7 5 3 1
This book has been cataloged with the Library of Congress.
ISBN 978-1-5344-2694-8 (paperback)
ISBN 978-1-5344-2695-5 (hardcover)
ISBN 978-1-5344-2696-2 (eBook)

CONTENTS

CHAPTER ONE

THE PURPLE MILKSHAKE

When it comes to school cafeterias, I've learned that they are always a mystery. Sometimes they are great! Sometimes they are the grossest places in the world. The problem is that you never know which one you'll get until you eat there.

See? That's me . . . not eating the most horrible food ever.

ANDRES MIEDOSO

But that all changed when I moved to Kersville. The cafeteria here at Kersville Elementary is one of a kind.

The food is excellent, according to my best friend, Desmond Cole. Whether it's Macaroni-and-Cheese Monday or Fried-Chicken Friday, the food always makes him happy.

So do the cafeteria workers. They must really like Desmond because they always give him extra food. They even make him special treats. One time they made a purple milkshake just for him.

I don't know what made it purple, and I didn't ask!

Desmond thinks the cafeteria is perfect. But my parents always say: If something seems too good to be true, it probably is. That's what I thought about my new cafeteria: It seemed too good to be true.

If only I knew how right I was!

DESMOND COLE

CHAPTER TWO

MRS. TRAY

It all started on a Monday. We were on our way to the cafeteria, and I was carrying my lunch box.

"I will never understand why you keep bringing lunch from home," Desmond said. "I'm telling you, our cafeteria makes the best food."

"I like bringing my lunch," I told him. Plus, I really loved my lunch box. It had a fire-breathing dragon on it.

Then Desmond added, "Well, the food here is way better than anything my parents make."

Desmond's parents were really great people, but there was one thing they weren't so great at: cooking. It was no wonder he liked the cafeteria food better.

"Well, you haven't tried my mom's empanadas," I said. Empanadas were my all-time favorite thing to eat ever since I was a little kid.

As soon as we reached the lunch-room, Desmond grabbed a tray and got in line. I followed him and watched as the servers plopped mounds of food on his plate. I had to admit, everything looked really yummy.

When we got to the end of the line, we saw Mrs. Tray. She was in charge of the cafeteria. She was also one of the nicest grown-ups at our school.

Mrs. Tray sniffed the air. "Andres, what's that wonderful smell?"

"That's my mom's empanadas," I said proudly. "She puts lots of spices in them."

"They smell amazing," Mrs. Tray said. "You are one lucky boy."

"I know," I said, smiling.

Desmond carried his heavy tray over to one of the empty tables. When he set it down, it made a loud *THUD*. He had a lot of food!

As he dug in, I opened my lunch box and unwrapped the crescent-shaped pies. They were stuffed full of meat and vegetables. I started to drool as the spicy smell hit my nose.

Even Desmond stopped eating to take a whiff.

"Do you want a bite?" I asked him.
"No, thanks," he said. "I have more than enough here." He went back to eating.

That was when I heard something strange. It sounded like a pair of wings flapping over my head, but when I looked up, there wasn't anything there.

Suddenly, Mrs. Tray was right next to me. She took another sniff of my empanadas, then started cleaning up my lunch. It was nice of her, but the only problem was, I wasn't finished eating yet!

Then she grabbed my empanada, but I held on tight.

"Mrs. Tray, I'm still eating my lunch," I explained.

With a strange look Mrs. Tray let go and apologized. Then she marched into the cafeteria's kitchen through a set of swinging doors.

As the doors swung open, I thought I saw something. It was a very, very, very hairy arm. And that very, very, very hairy arm was *purple*!

Before I could get a better look, Desmond tapped my shoulder. "Hey, are you going to finish that last empanada?"

"Um," I said, but it was too late. Desmond reached into my lunch box and snagged my empanada.

I was quick enough to save my food from Mrs. Tray, but I had to be a lot faster to beat Desmond Cole!

CHAPTER THREE

I SMELL MONSTERS

The next morning I was excited to see my dad making a chicken salad sandwich for my lunch. He uses a secret ingredient. He cuts up green grapes and mixes them in.

It looks like a regular sandwich until you bite into it.

Then it's a sweet and chicken-y flavor explosion in your mouth. I couldn't wait for lunchtime!

I grabbed my lunch box, hooked it on to my backpack, and headed to the garage to get my bike.

Only I wasn't alone in the garage. Zax was already there. He's the ghost that lives in my basement.

Believe me, that's something I never thought I'd say.

"Andres, can I ask you something?" Zax said.

"Okay, but make it fast," I told him. "I need to get to school."

Zax nodded and said, "Have you been hanging out with monsters?"

Me? Andres Miedoso? Hanging out with monsters? Ha!

I laughed out loud. "Impossible! There's no such thing as monsters . . . right?"

All of a sudden I wasn't so sure anymore. I mean, there I was talking to a ghost. Anything was possible in Kersville.

What if I had been hanging out with monsters without knowing it? Maybe monsters were really good at hiding. Maybe monsters were able to make themselves look like regular kids one minute and then change into ugly beasts the next. I didn't know.

"Zax," I said, "is there a way to know if I've been around monsters?"

"Oh, trust me. You would know," Zax replied. "Monsters have a very strong odor. If you haven't smelled anything funny, then you're good."

Phew! Good. Zax had me worried.

But I was *not* thrilled to know that monsters were real.

I climbed on my bike and was about to pedal off when I stopped.

"Hey, Zax," I said. "Why did you ask about monsters?"

"Oh, simple," he said. "Because I smell monsters all over you."

That was when I fell off my bike.

CHAPTER FOUR

THE ELM STREET HOUSE

I rode my bike to school extra fast that day.

Why?

Because I smelled like monsters. And if I smelled like monsters, that meant there were monsters close by.

Close to me!

I swallowed hard and pedaled harder. *How in the world could I smell like monsters?* I wondered. *It didn't make any sense.*

I rounded the corner onto Elm Street and saw the big house I passed every day. It was creepy-looking, even in the daytime. The gray paint was peeling, and the big windows had broken panes. There was no way anyone normal lived there.

Trees surrounded the house, and their branches crisscrossed in front like they were trying to hide the whole place. The house looked dark and scary.

I stopped to get a good look behind all those branches. *If monsters are in Kersville, they would totally live here*, I thought. And maybe that's

why I smelled like them! Like I said, I passed this house *every day*.

As I stood there, trying to spot any monsters in the windows, the street got quiet. My leg was shaking and my mouth was hanging open, but I couldn't help it. I was looking for monsters *and* hoping I wouldn't see any at the same time.

Finally, I realized I had to go. I
didn't want to be late for school. So I
took off again on my bike!

As I sped down the street fast,
I wondered if Zax was crazy. Or
maybe he was just pulling my leg.

By the way, that didn't mean what it sounded like. It was just another way of saying that Zax might have been teasing me.

Well, two can play that game!

I was thinking of a way to get back at Zax when I heard that same odd sound from the cafeteria yesterday. It sounded like wings flapping and swooping overhead.

I picked up speed, but the sound followed me. And that's when I saw it: A black shadow streaked across the ground and flew right behind me!

Then something grabbed my back-pack and wouldn't let go! The shadow was trying to pull me off my bike.

Quickly, I did the only thing I could think of: I swerved off the road and crashed into the prickliest briar bush I could find.

The shadow yowled and let go. To be honest I yowled too because OUCH! Turns out, crashing into a

briar bush wasn't the best idea in the world!

Still, it worked. I had scared off that shadowy monster, or whatever it was.

I checked my backpack, but there wasn't a scratch on it. My lunch box, on the other hand, was another story.

My favorite lunch box was completely wrecked.

CHAPTER FIVE

SPILLING THE BEANS

As soon as I got to school, I had to tell Desmond what happened. It's not every day you're attacked by a shadow monster! But we were way too busy in class, and there was really no time to talk.

So, I had to wait until lunch.

Let me tell you—it was really hard to hold on to a secret that huge for such a long time.

In the cafeteria line I whispered to Desmond, "I have to tell you what happened to me on the way to school this morning."

"Okay," he said. "But not right now. It's Taco Tuesday!"

"This is important!" I said.

That was when Mrs. Tray came over to us. "Hello, boys," she said. "My, what happened to your lunch box, Andres?"

"It's a long story," I said, and there was no way I was going to tell her. She wouldn't believe it anyway.

Still, Mrs. Tray stared at my lunch box. "What did you bring for lunch today?"

"My dad's chicken salad sandwich," I said. "He has a secret ingredient."

"Well, it smells wonderful," she said. I thought she was going to walk away to talk to some other kids, but she didn't. She just stood there, staring and sniffing!

I hope she doesn't try to grab my food again, I thought.

While Desmond got his lunch, I whispered to him, "Hurry up. We have to talk. I have—"

That was when Mrs. Tray interrupted me again. "So, what's the secret ingredient? Black olives? Yellow curry? Green peppers?"

"I can't tell anyone," I said. "Or it won't be a secret anymore."

Finally, Desmond turned around with a mountain of tacos. We found a table where we could talk alone. That was when I spilled the beans . . . like for real. I spilled the beans from one of Desmond's tacos!

It was an accident, but at least I'd gotten his attention.

After I cleaned up the mess, I told Desmond what Zax had said about monsters. And I told him about being attacked by a shadow on the way to school.

Talking about it made me start to feel scared all over again.

"Whoa," Desmond said, putting his taco down. "That's a crazy story!"

I knew he meant it. Desmond doesn't put his food down for just anything. But he *loves* mysteries! That's exactly why he started the Ghost Patrol!

"I know what we should do," said Desmond. "Let's talk to Zax after school. Maybe he can help us find these monsters. We need to see what they want."

"Uh, um, uh . . . ," I started, not sure I really wanted to *find* the monsters. But I knew Desmond wouldn't drop this until he had all the answers. "I—I guess so," I said.

I unwrapped my chicken salad sandwich. It had survived the attack of the shadow monster and the bike crash, but it was super-duper squished. I took a bite. Luckily, it still tasted great!

Good thing too. If Desmond was serious about finding the monsters, it might just be my last meal!

CHAPTER SIX

ROTTED LUCK

On the way home, Desmond and I rode our bikes to the mystery house on Elm Street. I don't want to say we were snooping. We were just curious. *Really* curious.

Oh, all right, we were snooping. Can you blame us?

We got off our bikes and looked up at the big house. Even though it was a sunny afternoon, there were thick clouds overhead and heavy fog surrounding the house. *Only* that house.

It was so weird.

Desmond took a deep breath and pushed open the rickety fence.

"W-wait," I said. "What are you doing?"

"We have to get closer," Desmond said.

He was perfectly calm, but I wasn't. I was already as close as I ever wanted to get to that house.

"Come on," Desmond said.

We walked up the path, which was covered with weeds and fallen branches. When we got to the house, there were four steps in front, but the wood was rotted and bendy. We had to climb them very carefully.

The house was even creepier up close. Now I could see the spider-webs covering the broken windows. When I looked inside, it was all pitch black except for one candle glowing in the corner of the dark, dark room.

"No monsters here," I said quickly. "I think it's time to go home."

I knew what Desmond was going to say before he opened his mouth. "No way. If there are monsters in Kersville, then we need to know what they're up to."

My heart dropped. Even if monsters didn't live here, Desmond wasn't going to give up his search.

So, we did what we had to do. We walked around the whole house, and man, was that hard. The weeds were so thick and so tall, it was like we were in a forest. That yard hadn't seen a lawn mower in *forever*!

"I hope we don't get lost back here," I said, laughing. "Nobody would ever find us."

"I know," Desmond said. "These weeds are taller than me!"

Just then the
sweetest smell in
the world drifted
through the air.
It smelled like
apples and sugar
and cinnamon—like

the freshest and yummiest baked
apple pie that ever existed.

And the smell was coming from
inside the house!

Desmond walked back toward the
front door without even saying anything. He looked like he was under a
spell or something.

I followed Desmond as he walked back up the rotted steps. Slowly, the front door opened. And yes, it made a very scary creaking sound, of course.

But you will never guess who opened the door.

Never!

It was Mrs. Tray! "Well, I'll be. Desmond? Andres? What are you boys doing here at my home?"

My eyes were opened wide, and I was too surprised to say anything.

Luckily, Desmond Cole was quick, quick, quick. "We were, uh, riding home when we smelled something delicious!" he said. "Are you baking a pie?"

Mrs. Tray smiled. "As a matter of fact, I am," she said. "I'm testing out a new pie recipe for school."

Then she just stood there and didn't say anything else. She was so quiet, we could hear those juicy pies baking.

Desmond looked at Mrs. Tray, studying her. But I just wanted to get out of there. Sure, Mrs. Tray was nice, but I did not want her to invite us into her super-creepy home.

I broke the silence and said, "I can't wait to try your new pie at school one day." Then I grabbed Desmond's arm. "Unfortunately, Desmond and I have to run now."

And that's just what we did.
Run!

CHAPTER SEVEN

MONSTERS LOVE TO EAT

Back at my house, we went up to my room. Zax was on my bed, reading one of my books. *Is this what he does all day?* I asked myself.

I closed the door behind us and said, "Zax, you have to tell us what you know about monsters!"

The ghost sat up. Or rather, he kind of *floated* up. "No problem," he said. "Well, the first thing you should know is that monsters love to eat. And they love kids."

I gulped and tried to keep myself from freaking out. "D-do you mean they love to eat *kids*?" My voice cracked when I asked the question.

Both Zax and Desmond gave me a look that said, "Cool it, Andres."

So I tried to relax.

Zax explained himself. "Monsters love eating food. They also love kids, but not to eat. No, no, no. Kids taste gross."

Desmond and I glanced at each other. *How would Zax know what kids taste like?*

Actually, I didn't want to know!

Then Zax continued. "You know, monsters are nothing like what you see in the movies. Real monsters hang out in large groups, not by themselves. But they don't want humans to see them. You wouldn't either if you had fangs, claws, and fur all over your body."

Desmond and I nodded. That made sense.

Zax floated all around Desmond. "Wow! You smell like monsters too."

Desmond sniffed under his arm. "What do monsters smell like?"

"Gross," Zax said as he held his ghost nose. "They smell like pencil erasers after you've just used them."

All of a sudden I could smell the monsters on Desmond too. He smelled kind of burny and kind of sweet at the same time. It was exactly like the smell of just-used erasers.

Desmond sniffed me and nodded. I must smell like monsters too.

As we sniffed each other, Zax sighed and said, "You humans are weird."

Desmond and I didn't care. We had bigger things to worry about than what one ghost thought about us.

There were monsters in Kersville. And it was up to the Ghost Patrol to find them!

CHAPTER EIGHT

DARK AND EARLY

Desmond and I had a really good plan. The only bad part was that we had to get up at the crack of dawn the next morning. Oh, and we had to hunt monsters.

I left my house with my backpack and scratched-up lunch box.

At Desmond's house, it was bright and early. Well, the sun hadn't even come up yet, which meant it was actually *dark* and early.

But we had a mission. Desmond unfolded a map of Kersville.

"Okay," he said. "I've put stars on all the places monsters would probably hang out. We can start at the garbage dump."

"Okay," I said. "But wait. Why did you put a star next to the car wash?"

Desmond shrugged. "I figured that's where monsters take showers."

I laughed. "Well, I guess it couldn't hurt to look there."

A half hour later we had checked all the stars on Desmond's map. There were no monsters anywhere. The sun was rising, and I knew that Desmond was worried we might not find anything scary.

But then, behind the museum, we saw it. A monster! It was peeking out from a fence. We could see its face with its huge round eyes and sharp pointy teeth. Its head looked hard, like it was made out of stone.

Desmond and I rode around the side of the building to see the rest of it, and—

It wasn't a monster at all. It was a large, ancient mask on a stand that was going into the museum.

"Oh man!" Desmond said. He was disappointed.

"That's not a monster, but it is a cool mask," I told Desmond. "We have to ask our teacher to bring us to the museum for our next class trip."

Desmond kicked a clump of dirt. "I guess" was all he said.

We started riding to school as the day was getting brighter. I smiled because at least we weren't going to find monsters that morning. Then we heard something weird. It sounded like a deep growl.

And the sound was getting closer and closer.

Desmond and I jumped off our bikes and hid behind some bushes. My heart was pounding as the growl got louder and louder.

Then . . . I heard Desmond laugh.
I opened my eyes as a motorcycle
drove by.

It was so loud, my teeth vibrated. I
let out a sigh. What was I expecting,
a monster on a motorcycle?

All this talk about monsters was making my imagination run wild.

It ran so wild that I thought I saw a monster across the street. It was blue and furry with giant monster teeth and dark sunglasses. And it was standing right in front of Sandy's Candies, the best candy store in Kersville.

"Okay, I need some sleep," I said. "I'm dreaming about monsters when I'm awake."

Desmond laughed. "You're not dreaming!"

We stared at each other. Now that we found a monster, what were we supposed to do? Of course, Desmond walked over to it, and I followed behind him . . . *way* behind him!

"Excuse me, monster," Desmond began. "We were wondering, um, what you want here in Kersville."

I hid behind Desmond, trying to force my body to stop shaking. I peeked over his shoulder, waiting to hear what the monster would say.

The monster looked at us and pulled off its head. Well, not really its head. It was more of a mask because the monster wasn't a monster. It was Zax in a costume!

"Got ya!" the ghost said, laughing.

Desmond laughed too, but I was too busy trying to remember how to breathe. "That's not *funny*, Zax!" I screamed.

Who would have thought I'd get stuck with a ghost who liked to play jokes on me? Just my luck!

I checked my watch. Jokes or not, it was almost time for school. When we got to Kersville Elementary, we must have been the first kids there.

"Hey, we are early enough for breakfast," Desmond said. "This will give us time to figure out where those monsters are hiding."

We went to the cafeteria and grabbed trays. The servers dumped spoonfuls of food on our plates, but Desmond and I weren't really paying attention. We had our heads buried in the map.

That was when it happened.

A smell hit my nose. And no, it wasn't the food.

Desmond and I looked at each other, and our eyes grew wider. We both smelled the same thing.

SNIFF!

SNIFF

It was a little *burny*.
And a little *sweet*.
Just like an *eraser*!
That's when we knew. We weren't
the only ones who had come to school
early that day!

SNIFF!

SNIFF!

105

CHAPTER NINE

CATCH-A-TONY

Desmond dropped the map, and we finally looked around. Wow, did we find what we had been looking for! There were monsters *everywhere*! All kinds of monsters at every table. And let me tell you, they were the messiest eaters I'd ever seen.

They were even messier than the kids at Kersville Elementary. And that's saying something! There were globs and globs of gross food everywhere!

Desmond and I froze in place when a giant winged creature swooped down from above. It was the same thing that had followed me before.

It was that shadow monster!

And just like last time, it went right for my tray.

Then it circled back and grabbed my lunch box. My *abuela*'s special noodle soup was in there. It was sweet and spicy, and there was no way I was going to let some monster tear it away from me.

So I fought back. The next thing I knew, we were in a tug-of-war.

I learned an important lesson that day: Never play tug-of-war with a winged beast. Just don't do it!

Before I knew it, he had pulled me into the air! We zoomed around the

lunchroom while the monsters kept eating their food, splattering glop all over the place. I mean, didn't they know anything about table manners?

Me? My mouth was open almost as wide as my eyes, but I was too scared to scream.

That's when I noticed Desmond. He had climbed on top of a table and was reaching out to try and grab me. When I got close enough, he wrapped his arms around my legs, but before he could pull me down, we were *both* flying around in the air.

The monsters beneath us were almost finished with their food. I just hoped we wouldn't be their *dessert*!

If we were going to escape, it was now or never. I pulled down on my lunch box, and the strap snapped.

Desmond and I fell . . . and landed right on a pile of goop. It was filled with apple cores, pencil shavings, and toenail clippings.

It. Was. The. Worst.

I almost threw up, but that wasn't going to help things at all.

A huge purple monster stood right in front of us. I held my breath because the goop smelled really gross and because I was scared. This was it. We were going to be eaten!

The monster picked us up by our feet. Then it said, "Mrs. Tray, we have a little pest problem."

Mrs. Tray opened the kitchen's swinging doors. "Desmond? Andres? You are both here early."

"Um, Mrs. Tray," Desmond said. "Can you explain what's going on?"

Mrs. Tray smiled and turned to the purple monster. "Catch-a-Tony," she said to it in a sweet voice, "can you please put these students down?"

"All right," Catch-a-Tony said. He released us, and we fell back into the goop.

Mrs. Tray turned to the rest of the monsters. "Okay, helpers, the school is opening soon. It's time to clean up this mess and start cooking lunch for the kids. Remember, it's cheese-burger day!"

As the monsters started cleaning up and putting on aprons, Desmond and I sat there on the newly cleaned floor. I could tell by looking at him that something big had happened.

Desmond Cole had officially lost his appetite.

CHAPTER TEN

MONSTER MENU

It turns out that all those delicious cafeteria meals Desmond loved were made by monsters. Mrs. Tray is in charge of the kitchen, but the monsters are the true master chefs!

Every morning Mrs. Tray makes food for the monsters.

And she always makes them really gross stuff. Their favorite breakfast is oatmeal topped with green boogers and dead flies.

Like I said, *gross*!

When they finish eating they clean up and start cooking in the kitchen. After work they head home together, to that weird house on Elm Street.

Yes, they all live there with Mrs. Tray!

As for that one monster who kept attacking me? Well, his name is Paul. And he wasn't trying to hurt me. He just wanted the food in my lunch box. Not to eat, of course. Monsters wouldn't eat anything that normal. Paul said my food smelled so good

that he wanted to figure out the recipe so he could add it to the school menu!

I'm just happy to know Paul wasn't trying to eat *me*!

So now Desmond and I have a big secret, and we can't tell anyone about it. 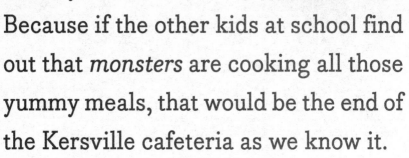 Because if the other kids at school find out that *monsters* are cooking all those yummy meals, that would be the end of the Kersville cafeteria as we know it.

And nobody wants that!